自 序
深呼吸 擁抱不完美

賣夢日記是當年在人生谷底面對著脆弱和痛苦，
發現自己迫切需要在自然裡呼吸，
而在舊賣夢工作室臨時的自然場域裡發生的所感所記……
過了這麼多年，
想要再重新整理與出版分享，
做為滋養自己生命重整的回顧力量，
也透過文字或圖片傳遞溫柔慈悲陪伴自己的力量，
分享給打開此日記的有緣人，
願以愛觸動溫暖每個有緣生命～

此時此刻的我，
回看 2013 年的療癒日記，
一切已物換星移，
充滿豐盛與美好的轉變，
無論喜悲，
無論好或是不好，
而我還是我；
不同的是，
我學會了帶著覺知為選擇負責勇往前行，
溫柔慈悲的陪伴每一個狀態中的自己，
也適時的尋求支持！

在第 14 頁大寒日記裡提到「我討厭阿爸的說公益」、
「魚翅」的內容是當時的心情抒發及主觀想法，
而後來的多年以來，
我親愛的阿爸一樣跟我在某些觀念與作為上是平行宇宙，
卻是我在服務土地及公益活動分享中最投入的志工和最大的贊助者，
我心存感謝，
也享受跟爸爸的合作，
比如說：當我提到種菜下農藥對人類土地的危害，
阿爸學習改變種菜習慣停用農藥多用自然肥與土地共生共好；
當我開始向樹的生命力學習，
這些年阿爸用行動在舊賣夢場域種下 2000 顆樹苗，
無形中實現了復育森林，
我心裡充滿感動。
我發現我的傻瓜精神來自阿爸，
謝謝阿爸的傻瓜精神，
讓愛流動，
做就對了！

生命是一場喜悅在主導的慶典，
祝福地球自然與人自在豐盛和平和諧共處，
無論喜悲享受生命如此珍貴而美好！

魏世芬

《你擁有夢嗎，在夢中你會唱歌、跳舞、畫圖、說故事嗎？》

每晚入睡前，我都會興奮得期待，過幾分鐘後，閉上眼，穿越深沉的呼吸，我就可以和夢中的自己重逢。

在睡前，希望我可以釋放每天工作的壓力、憂慮，與人相會的快樂或開心，歸零。

在現實生活中你有夢想嗎？有沒有想過，夢中的你大膽奔放，無所不能，但醒來之後，真實的夢想又被壓抑了，如果你能在睡前釋放你每天的黑黑、疲倦、壓力，對自己的否定，是否你可以修復還原你的力量。

看著這一本賣夢日記，真實的領取自己每天的不同情緒，把它說出來、畫出來，從呼吸中釋放出來。

期待你們跟我一樣享受日記中每一個故事、心情及美好片刻，成為一個有夢的人。

推薦文

推開心窗，迎向生命之光。

楊忠衡

音樂時代劇場藝術總監

每個人來到世間的第一刻，就開始學習生活、體驗生命。
過程中，我們可能得到父母與師長的指導，
也可能得到智者哲人的啟發，甚或寄託於宗教的指引。

然而我們是否忽略，其實呵護、哺育著我們的，
是最親近我們，靜默的大自然。

當我們敞開心胸，取得與自然、宇宙的聯結，就可以得到不可言喻的共鳴。
無限的慈悲、寬憫、與愛，本來就存在我們靈魂裡，只是期待著開發出來的密因。

本書是作者 Dreamer 自我療癒的生活手記。
這些或長、或短的文字與圖片，看來像是隨機捕捉的生活感懷，
或是靈光乍現的領悟。但它就是一段與天地、自然交流的無偽歷程。

「讓賣夢的自然呼吸，幫自己推開心窗，想夢；造夢；讓夢想力修復，轉動。」

這段療癒過程帶給 Dreamer 莫大的啟發，也是她的人生轉捩點。
我感佩於 Dreamer 找到心靈解脫的路，不是經過外人指導，
而是得自內心的「悟」。
就像無意識間，上天交到手裡的禮物。

Dreamer 忠實記下這個過程，像一段心靈遊記。
透過本書，她邀請您一起走過。
建議您以安適順緣的心閱讀，
也許哪段吉光片羽，也能開啟您的心窗，
一窺閃爍其中的生命之光。

推薦文

見證生命的識讀與奇蹟

凌春玉

格致視覺藝術學習塾總監

Dreamer 抱定的一個不凡信念，就是始終確信有意識地自我認同，有助於呈現自然療癒力量背後的真正價值。《賣夢日記》是一本自我療癒的生活札記，她試圖打開 2013~2014 年的「時光寶盒」，分享關於如何閱讀自己如何尊重宇宙與靈性共好之經歷與過程，其中包括了藝術、療癒、教育、社會服務等在大自然運作中的共修體驗，並如何從概括地承受與『善念』的相互包容。

生命是一場充滿多樣性的覺知與感恩！從中深入地尊敬生物的多樣化，以柔性的力量支持自我修復，並將挑戰的過程表述為生命歷程的察覺。書中赤裸裸地描述 Dreamer 如何在病識中，有意識地「陪伴自己」與進行深層地「自我對話」。藉由一次次的「與自然對話」以及「認同自我」，從而打開夢想力。

期盼本書能讓更多讀者領略其中的視覺跡象，逐漸進入思想的樂趣。透過個人經驗之分享，進化至精神與意識的層次；如何專注傾聽生命體的投射，並好好善待自己。進而啟動善念並轉變自我的生活方式。文中揭露她獨特「愛自己」的方法，講述她在二十四節氣中自療的經歷過程，進行本我意識覺知與靈念的心流使愛轉動。

生活就應自然簡單，過多的負荷讓生活陷入困境，藉由深呼吸、擁抱不完美、讓愛流動，從而積極建構出生命的多元體驗。希望透過對於日常的識讀力 (Literacy)，讀者有更多機會「看見」和「讀出」Dreamer 的思維與智慧，從中幫助自己做出有效的判斷與更好的構想。突破認知的限制與世俗框架，回歸自己、發現自己、陪伴自己、進而擁抱生命、熱愛自己！這猶如一道具有閃光、創造時代的宏觀視野，使人懷著謙卑與喜悅的本性，專注地對自身溝通交流，落實在行動中感受，期待遇見更好得自己！

目　錄

自　序　002

推薦序　003-006

本　文　008-055

2012 年是開始賣夢的起點，
而賣夢日記是作者 Dreamer 在舊賣夢場域中，
階段性的日常書寫，
透過在生命中整理生命的過程與大家分享，
2022 年特別以二十四節氣的方式編排回憶阿爸森林的一切，
而作者的女兒彤，
也在原有的日記中加上對話框與過去母親的日常對話，
讓賣夢日記更加生動活躍，
希望讀到本書的有緣人都能遇見未知的自己。

記憶改寫，創造幸福。課程後，此刻的疲憊是什麼？

我在其中，在找什麼？我，卻又感覺一點都不想再找什麼了…

昨晚舞蹈治療的鬆綁感，真好。

人生，總被框架了要活出意義，而意義，也已經被定義好。

我，可以只是單純的活著，感受世界的美好與分享那份體會的美好嗎？

Recreate your memory to create happiness. Where does that weariness come from after class?

I am in it, but what am I looking for? I don't feel like searching anymore.

Last night's dance therapy released me. It felt so good.

We're told to search for a meaningful life. But the meaning of life is defined by others.

Can I simply be alive, enjoying the beauty of the earth and sharing my realization about life?

練習感受每一個當下的美好。

Being in the moment, appreciating here and now.

賣夢小花園

迷迭香
醒腦、促進血液循環。

人生是被一堆狗屁狗尿包裹著的。

我討厭阿爸的『說公益』。我永遠不會在今生的框架裡實現我內心的想望的。

因為，我被賦予『活在說裡面，不是活著做就對了』～

這世界，總是一群集體恐懼的人們，

學會用看得到的名『頭銜、金錢、鑽石、限量的名牌、珍貴的食物《魚翅…》』來填補內心的恐懼與潰乏。

就像神隱少女裡的貪吃的爸媽，吃到變豬，就只是知道吃，回不到人本世界了…

我輸了。我永遠就是輸家。我一點都不想醒來。。

【彤貼心的帶水豚君來為我傾聽，讓我把把，陪我哭，謝謝彤。】

Life is full of crap.

I hated it when Dad talked about doing good deeds. I would never fulfill my desire in this life because I am brainwashed by Dad's chatter that "to say is to live and you need not do anything."

There is mass hysteria everywhere. People are accustomed to using material items, such as titles, money, diamonds, limited edition or delicacies, to fill the emptiness and lessen the uneasiness.

Just like in the movie Spirited Away where Chihiro's parents have an insatiable desire for food, all they ever care about is food to the point that they eventually become pigs and would never return to human form again. I will be a loser for the rest of my life if I lose. I have no desire to wake up.

(A sweet girl, Tong, brought Kapibarasan to visit me. She listened to me, hugged me, and cried with me. I really appreciated her kindness.)

別只是光說不做，不要懷疑，相信自己，做就對了！

Actions speak louder than words. Don't doubt. Believe in yourself. Just do it.

賣夢小花園 　香蜂草

鎮靜、解熱、緩解喉嚨痛。

農曆年前，大多數的人們，收拾行囊出發，是為回家返鄉，而我收拾行囊出發，是遠離家，
遠離居住的城市，「心」，卻是急著想回心的家。。

一生中，究竟哪些夢想可以真實去實現，而哪些是鏡花水月，需要遠離保持安全與平靜的人生？？
或許根本沒有安全的答案，只有遇到了，就讓它過去吧！

那麼，如果一輩子都住在海市蜃樓中呢？。。嗯，就想夢吧！只要不傷害自己不傷害他人，

我就好好想一個聯結宇宙發電機，推自己回歸內在平衡，讓自己開心的『紫樓夢』(_*_^_。_^_*_)_

把我最愛的紫色放入夢樓中實現圓夢。認識此生緣起，也同時放下緣滅。心且生滅隨緣，自在無礙。
然後，歡迎，也拐倒在海市蜃樓前的尋夢人，進來呼吸修復一下。

With Chinese New Year's Eve coming, people are busy packing and returning home for a big reunion.
However, I am busy packing and going away from home, leaving the city I grew up. My heart is eager to find its way home.

How many dreams can be realized throughout one's lifetime? How can one identify which dreams are worthy of pursuing
and which to disregard? Should I go for it and not care about leaving my comfort zone and current peaceful life? There
may be no such thing as a safe bet. Once you encounter it, you should just let it go.

What if we choose to live in the castle in the air?
I dare you to dream as long as you are not hurting yourself and others. I allow myself to dream about the universe
delivering me a generator to push me back to my inner balance. This is a happy Dream of Purple Mansion.

Put my favorite color, purple, in the mansion of my dream to fulfill my desire.
Understand that phenomena arise when conditions are present and cease when such conditions scatter.
My heart sets out to go with the flow of situations, so I am completely at ease without constraints.

Welcome, all the dream seekers who tumbled in front of the castle in the air.
Please come inside and take a breath to relax for a while.

每個人的心中都住著一個小天使，天使的翅膀供應我們一個避雨的遮蔽處，
在那裡我可以得到片刻的寧靜，休息、整頓自己～（也可以來賣夢坐坐）

An angel is living inside everyone's heart. Angel wings act as the umbrella shielding us from the rain and providing us with a space to chill and collect ourselves.(You are welcomed to the House of Dreams to chat and chill.)

賣夢小花園

土肉桂
防止腹瀉、反胃、嘔吐等等⋯。

感受生命的無常～什麼是我們該珍惜，該去努力的？

生活索事，不知不覺常成了自困的困局，該如何捨斷，才得心安自在？

是需要不斷練習重來的過程，並從中觀照心路，當照見心路的軌跡，也就是突破困局的生機⋯

今天是個默哀日⋯到賣夢呼吸⋯看見賣夢牆上，有位朋友的留言『想把心留在這裡』⋯

想說：謝謝你喜歡賣夢呼吸大教室，相信在這裡，你的靈魂跟我一樣鬆綁與自由。

更要祝福你，帶著在賣夢所呼吸到的解靈能量，為自己的生命旅途努力創造幸福⋯

Life is full of uncertainties. What should we cherish? What should we pursue?

We are constantly obsessed with daily trivia without noticing it's all self-inflicted.
How can we get rid of old stuff to attain a peaceful mind?

It requires a process of practicing and do-over. You learn how to be mindful of the changes in your thought. Once you can see clearly your spiritual path, the chance to overcome difficulties is budding.

Today is for silent tribute. I went to the House of Dreams to breathe and saw a friend leave a message on the wall stating, "I want to leave my heart here."

I want to say to him," thank you for enjoying your time in the House of Dreams. I believe when you are here, your soul is relaxed and free of boundaries, just like me.

Since you've unlocked your inner energy here,
you should be able to create a life full of happiness and abundance. I wish you all the best.

活在當下，感受每一天自己的身、心狀態，就是活在當下。帶著覺知、帶著愛～

Living in the moment. Being mindful of your body and soul equals being present.

想留在這裡
把心留在這裡

賣夢小花園　艾草
防止蟲害、烹煮食用。

什麼記憶值得一輩子？什麼是真故事？什麼是虛構情節？
想想，『恐懼』是什麼時候被故事化，而無形的入侵生活中，影響人生？

今天，專注再聽聽小姑姑的恐怖故事。。從故事中，窺見小時候的姑姑很會為自己『找樂子』，
不到田裡工作，跑去看歌仔戲，跑去看娶新娘鬧洞房，回家因為天黑，很恐懼的走黑路回家，
不被媽媽安慰因怕黑的恐懼，還會被指責。。

今天忘了抱抱姑姑，秀秀她的小時候感受恐懼時，還被阿嬤責備的委屈…

『姑，謝謝你耐性的說故事，也祝福你的內心所累積的恐懼不再。
都過去了…祝福你天天開心…(＿*＿^＿o＿^＿*＿)』

What memories are worth bearing in mind for the rest of our lives?
What is a true story, and what is fabrication? Think about it, when did fear infiltrate our story, then gradually
infiltrate our daily activities and ultimately affect our life?

Today I listened to my aunt's horror stories once again. From the stories, I noticed that aunt was good at finding
small happiness, such as avoiding working in the field, going to Taiwanese opera, and crashing bedding ceremonies.
On her way home, she was terrorized because it was getting too dark to see. Instead of comforting her, her mother
scolded her for coming home late.

I forgot to hug my aunt today to soothe her fears and grievances from childhood memories.

Dear aunt, thank you for sharing your stories. I hope all the fears accumulated from your childhood will fade away
soon. It's all in the past, and I wish you happy every day.

當你覺察到過去的情緒時，邀請你用各種方式來秀秀他、抱抱他。

When you are aware of past traumas, hug yourself as if you are comforting
yourself in the past.

賣夢小花園　**德國洋甘菊**
抗菌、抗發炎、抗過敏。

年後遠行歸來的第一聚，

阿爸請來了四位姑姑還有許多子孫們來聚，很開心他們也來賣夢走春嘍～

兄弟姐妹的感情維繫，也都不盡相同，有共同成長的過程是好的，

路，也才能相扶持久久⋯

我，一個人，習慣了，也總不習慣；就是要記得將心中的愛流動出去，它，才會再長出來喔！

真的！我今天關愛一下親友後，心也跟著靜下來，就像賣夢的薰衣草般明亮寧靜。

I came back from the long trip after New Year just in time for the first family gathering this year.
Father invited my four aunts and other relatives. I was happy to see them visit the House of Dreams and giving New Year's greetings.

Relationships between brothers and sisters can be tricky; nevertheless, growing up with siblings and building a strong supportive network for each other is great.

I thought I was used to being alone by myself, but it turns out I will never be used to it. I need to remind myself to send out the love from my heart. The flow of love will produce more love inside me.

It's so true! With sending out love to my relatives and friends today, I felt calm and peaceful, like the bright lavender in the House of Dreams.

出去走走，跟人互動有益身體健康～

Going out and mingling helps to maintain a healthy body and mind.

賣夢小花園

茴香

增進食慾、促進消化。

賣夢的 _ 某角落，總是 _ 有些 _ 嚇一跳的 _ 伙伴，

假裝 _ 暗兵不動 _ 的觀察著彼此…我怕 _ 你，你 _ 怕我。。

恐懼 _，都來自哪裡呢？

每一次的 _ 學習擁抱 _ 恐懼，

與 _ 自己 _ 合作。源源不絕。

There are always some teammates lurking around the corners in the House of Dreams to surprise you, and sometimes not in a good way.

I sit tight and observe everyone's steps. We are all watching our backs.

Where does the fear come from? I try to embrace fear and cooperate with myself again and again, endlessly.

> **擁抱恐懼…好難…但值得挑戰～**
>
> **It's challenging to embrace fear, but it's also worth trying.**

賣夢小花園

甜萬壽菊
幫助消化、清熱、甜甜的味道。

留住我的愛～在生命的谷底時，除了痛覺，愛感覺不見了，

但它其實一直在，只是被心的痛覺掩蓋住了存在，

「唯有同理關懷，付出與分享的流動，會讓愛傳下去。」

分享與關懷會找回愛的力量 _，會把失落的愛保存留住～

以愛的力量造夢，感受與分享世界的美好。

Keep my love. I can only feel the pain when I hit rock bottom and all the love is gone.

But love never goes away. The feeling of pain is just covering it.

Only sympathy and care coupled with devotion and sharing then the love pay forward.

Sharing and caring will help you regain the power of love.

Use the power of love to pursue your dreams, appreciate the beauty of the world, and share it with others.

看看海、看看山、看看這個美麗的世界，讓愛流動～分享你今天的美好時刻吧。

Look at the sea, look at the mountains, and look at the beautiful world. Let love flow and share your wonderful moments of today.

賣夢小花園　**玫瑰天竺葵**
抗菌、抗憂鬱、似玫瑰的香氣。

隨緣渡。

生命河流, 總會不斷的隨河道順流而下,

延途的石頭, 枯枝, 雜物, 碰撞無數, 載浮載沉, 又不斷的被延途上經過的船接泊著, 安然無恙;

感恩順逆因緣渡, 成長我的心, 安住我的身, 引渡我的靈。

應無所住, 讓心安住。人生旅程續航著, 感恩有緣渡隨緣…

Go with the flow.

The flow of life is like a river, which always goes downstream.

While going ups and downs, bumping into the stones, deadwood, and all kinds of stuff, we will also be saved by the ships passing by and come out safe and sound.

Bitter or sweet, we shall appreciate the flow of life. It guides our soul to grow and to abide in that mental state.

Free your mind and rest for your soul. The life journey continues; we only need to appreciate every encounter and go with the flow.

每個人的心中都有佛，安住身心，就可以感受到內在的寧靜與安定，就從回到呼吸開始

Buddha lives in the hearts of believers. Abiding in that mental state and you will find inner peace. It all starts with breathing.

賣夢小花園

澳洲茶樹
幫助傷口癒合、防止細菌感染、殺菌。

腦袋像當機一樣好幾天。

昨夜夢中，見到自己的時空原來禁止了，而世界依然運轉。

也看到整體性的互相影響作用著，而我，停止就不受作用其擾了。

靜心，讓自己更肯定自己的路。

My brain has been shut down for several days.

Last night I dreamed that my time and space had been prohibited, but the rest of the world was still moving.

While dreaming, I also realized that everything is intertwined and affected by each other.

Once I was prohibited, I was free from all the interference.

> **時間不會因此停下，繼續前進吧。**
>
> Time will not stop moving, no matter what. Keep on going forward.

賣夢小花園　桂花
平衡神經系統、除口臭、健胃整腸。

午後阿爸問我有要去哪嗎？他想去二姑的菜園。於是，我跟去了一下。。

好久沒進姑姑的菜園了，看見多了好多的菜長大，
還意外將『瘋女人【台語發音】』的植物誤認為芹菜，

被姑姑笑 (_*_^_o_^_*_)_,

看見姑姑的菜園是更有鄉土味與資源再利用，她放好多桶子讓下雨水接住澆灌用，
姑姑是這塊土地第一個種菜的人，當時沒水，常常聽她跟著天氣喜與憂菜的狀況。

如今，阿爸已經導入水源，狀況好很多。
阿爸進到菜園就忙到處採收…真是歡暢的活動 (_*_^_o_^_*_)_

Father asked, "where are you going?" this afternoon.
He wanted to visit my aunt in the vegetable garden. So I went along with him.

It's been a long time since I last visited my aunt's garden. There is much more variety of plants growing. Aunt laughed at me when I mistook the small flower beggarticks as celery.

Aunt's garden makes me feel like I am in the countryside, and she implements several environmentally friendly applications, such as using several buckets to collect rainwater to irrigate the garden. Aunt was the first one to grow vegetables on this lot. Back then, she had to face the difficulty of water shortage, so her mood was up and down with the changing weather conditions.

Nevertheless, Father helped her to build an irrigation system and improved the overall conditions.
Today Father came to help harvest. What a joyful activity!

你有去過菜園嗎？菜園總是充滿驚喜喔！

Have you ever been to a vegetable garden? It's full of surprises.

賣夢小花園

九層塔

富含維生素Ａ、Ｃ、鈣…。

薄荷在水裡，一樣會長氣根而生生不息。

C_o_o_l_。

【水中薄荷根生而味淡】這個冬天，我也在冬眠。。

春生、夏長、秋收、冬藏。法自然。

Mint grows aerial roots in the water and continues its life circle.

It's cool.

Mint in the water grows root and tastes light. This winter, I will hibernate.

Plant in spring, grow in summer, harvest in fall, and rest in winter. That's the law of nature.

總能在植物身上看見無限的生命力、純粹的美。

I can always find the unlimited life force in plants. It's pure beauty.

賣夢小花園　　**薄荷**
可泡茶、提神醒腦。

將生命活的精彩極緻，就如同這薰衣草的盛開般的動人，

留住生命的精彩續集～

來吧！乾燥薰衣草。(＿＊＿＾＿。＾＿＊＿)＿

Live life to the fullest, just like the charming full-bloom lavender.

Preserve the beauty of life for a splendid sequel.

Come on, dried lavender!

紫色的薰衣草充滿著神秘的美，就像人生一般…。

Beautiful purple lavender is filled with mysteries, similar to life.

賣夢小花園　　　**薰衣草**
安眠、舒緩緊張。

彤顏純真～這療癒瑜珈～

彤每到一個體位動作就很快入眠～

真羨慕這入定的速度啊！

年輕真好 (_*_^_o_^_*_)_

Tong looks so innocent.

During the the yoga therapy class, whenever Tong arrived at an asana, she could quickly fell asleep.

I was envious of the fact that she could reach stillness so soon.

It's nice to be young.

能在瑜伽體位中休眠也是種幸福呀！

It's a blessing to shut down your mind during yoga practice.

賣夢小花園　紫蘇

促進食慾、消胃脹、利尿。

小學時就常一個人哭著自問，我為什麼生在這，為什麼世界上只有我有感覺，

唉…原來這感覺就是孤獨，是人與生俱來的，

我一直沒有承認它可以存在我生命中，

想想，不就好像不肯讓心臟跳動一樣為難自己…

「享受孤獨的自由。享受孤獨的寧靜。」

感恩肉體與靈魂相伴，雖孤獨亦滿足。知足亦幸福。

I was crying and asking myself often why I was here and the only one in this world with feelings since I was a kid.

Later I learned that this emotion is the so-called "loneliness." Human is born with loneliness.

I've never recognized that I could live with it. Giving it a second thought, I realized I had made my life difficult.

It's no different than trying to stop my heart from beating.

Enjoy the freedom of being alone. Enjoy the silence of being alone.

I appreciate my body and soul. I am lonely, but I am satisfied. Satisfying brings happiness.

每個人都來自宇宙的愛，告訴自己：我愛自己，也值得被愛。

**Every person was born out of love in this universe.
Tell yourself that I love myself and I am worthy of being loved.**

賣夢小花園　　魚腥草
抗菌、解毒、消腫痛。

好久沒合照了。

阿爸答應看彤演出前，一起用餐，聊到前天小姑姑提到的彰化故鄉，沒燈摸黑的恐怖兒時歲月，
原來阿爸也超怕…媽媽半夜要生大姐，爸爸不敢自己出去，是找小姑姑陪他出去找產婆的。。

我的怕黑，是來自爸爸家族的環境恐懼原始記憶嗎？

故鄉的黑夜，加上死亡的靈魂傳說，讓所有人相信了，害怕了…

忽然想：『電燈』的發明，不只是照明環境，也是給了大多數人免於黑暗的內在恐懼。

It was a long time ago when we took group photos.

Father promised to have dinner together before going to Tong's performance. We talked about our old house in Changhua City aunt mentioned several days ago. They grew up without electricity and had to endure the scary nighttime. It turned out Father was afraid of the dark. Mother had to give birth to my old sister, but Father feared going out alone. So he asked my aunt to go with him to find a midwife.

Is it because of the family history of environmental fear from my dad's side that I am also afraid of the dark?

The gloomy nights further convinced everybody that the ghost stories from my hometown were true. Everyone is frightened.

A thought came to my mind that the invention of electricity not only lights up the environment but also prevents us from evoking inner fear due to the darkness.

死亡並不可怕，可怕的是未知帶來的恐懼感，呼吸～回到當下。

What we are afraid of is not dying but the feelings of horror when facing the unknown. Breathe and come back to here and now

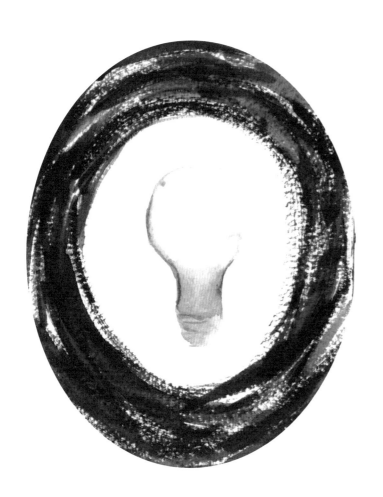

賣夢小花園 　羅勒
促進消化、舒解精神疲勞。

今天的第三樣第一次嚐試⋯油漆。

我親手將紫色的溫暖穿到灰冷的心牆上，

於是，心暖笑開了⋯過癮 (_*_^_o_^_*_)_

The third first experience today: is painting.

I painted the gray and cold walls around the heart with the warmth of purple.

My heart felt the warmth and smiled. It was so satisfying.

4
4

在白露這天，透過雙手親自塗抹油漆的回憶，紫色的油漆如同綻放的薰衣草，
溫柔不高調的美，現在回想起來心依舊暖暖的，你是否也有讓你想到就心暖的回憶呢
（該不會也在白露這天吧！?）

On the day of White Dew, the memory of painting the walls came alive.
Purple paint resembles the exuberant lavender expressing a tender and
elegant beauty. It still gives me a heartfelt warmth looking back at that
time. Do you have this kind of memory too? Maybe it's also on the day of
White Dew.

賣夢小花園　快樂鼠尾草

放鬆、舒緩、平衡。

阿爸，居然如此活力四射過⋯遺忘的阿爸的模樣，

阿爸，你自己曾經想起嗎？

四肢全開的自信與勇氣，真的好勇喔！(_*_^_o_^_*_)_

I can't believe that dad once was so energetic and vibrant. Some images of dad's past have faded away.

Dad, have you ever thought about the old times?

Your robust body was full of confidence and courage. It's so impressive!

年輕時的自信、天真模樣，現在依然在嗎？

Can you still find the confidence and innocence you possessed when you were young?

賣夢小花園　**柚子**
防便秘、含豐富維他命 c。

找阿爸的照片，卻找到阿母單獨與我的合照；

看我笑的燦爛，感覺到當下的幸福溫度…或許，每個當下，都該努力為自己心中的幸福溫度

找到加溫的方式，讓心中每個當下的幸福溫度保持恆溫…

I was looking for my dad's old photos; instead, I found a photo of my mom and me.

I smiled like a sunflower in the photo, and I can still sense the happiness at that moment.

We should create a happy memory in every moment to maintain a constant joyous mind and soul.

在這個當下有什麼事情讓你感到幸福呢？
尋找自己當下的幸福感（一杯咖啡）。

What makes you feel happy at this moment? A cup of coffee?
As long as you keep pursuing, you can live happily every second.

賣夢小花園

到手香（左手香）
消炎消腫、舒緩蚊蟲咬傷。

阿爸是山，在遙望的對岸邊，高高聳立不搖。

阿爸是山，盡力的、不斷的創造，涵養四週有緣，用之不竭。

阿爸永遠是遠處的高山，靜靜的聳立，穿越雲端。。。

Dad is like a mountain rising tall from a distance on the other side of the river.

Dad is like a mountain that tries to provide endless nutrients to nurture surrounding creatures.

Dad will always be the high mountain from a distance, standing silently and soaring into the sky.

5
0

做自己的山…

Be your own mountain.

賣夢小花園  苦楝

殺蟲、止癢。

其實我是自戀的。像灰姑娘般，一直尋找著屬於自己的舞台，
展現澎湃的熱情，又要準時變回原狀。

我期盼，我祝福，每個當下的好念，都匯聚成心靈存單，

在心靈定存時間到的時候，我將於歸屬的舞台上，
活力充沛，神采飛揚的讓自己豐收，同時也豐潤他人…

I am actually a bit full of myself. Like Cinderella, I keep looking for my own stage to showcase my talents and energy, but ready to go back to the normal me before midnight.

I expect and pray that every good intention in the present will accumulate and become an asset for my soul.

When the time is right, I'll be back on the stage with full energy to bring forth a spectacular performance to nourish the audience's soul while cultivating an abundant life for myself.

自戀點吧，看著鏡子裡的自己，對自己說：哈囉你真美 / 你真帥。

It's no harm to be a bit full of yourself. Look at yourself in the mirror, and say to yourself, "you are so charming."

賣夢小花園

芳香萬壽菊
提神醒腦、提升專注力、放鬆。

5
4

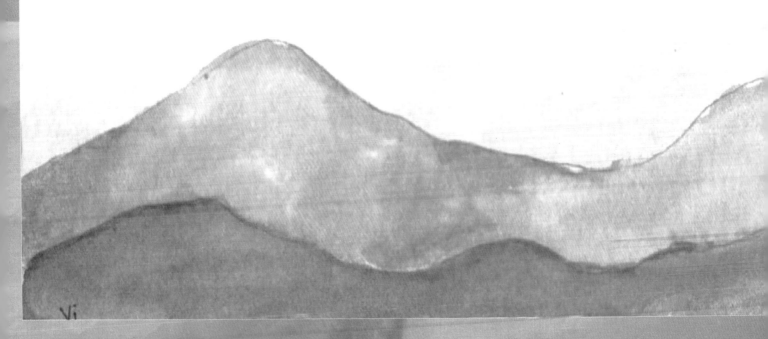

好天氣，眺望遠處的遼闊天際，

心，也隨之飛舞山林間，自在遨遊；感覺到山林萬物的欣悅蠢動，不斷的共鳴迴盪；

就這樣瞬間，我與自然共舞⋯

Cashing in on the fine weather,

I enjoy a broad horizon with my heart wandering around the mountains and the forests and listening to all the mountain creatures playing melodious tunes.

At that moment, I am dancing with nature.

偶而回到自然中充充電，能抱持身心的平衡呢。

Placing yourself in nature to recharge once in a while will give you a balanced body and mind.

賣夢小花園

檸檬桉

殺菌驅蟲、治療喉嚨痛。

起落人生，起落的心情。

好想停一停，不用再回應這世界的任何人事物，就只是大口的好好呼吸著。。

沒有比較、沒有阻力、擁有被尊重、可以圓自己的夢、累了就停、想到就做、沒有批判，

只有大口呼吸的暢快舒坦，自在飛翔。。多好啊！

Life goes up and down, and so does the mood.

I want to pause and not respond to anyone or anything. I need to focus on my breathing in and breathing out.

Without comparing, with hindrance, without judgments, we respect each other to go after our dreams.
We can stop anytime we want and start again once we feel ready.

The only thing that matters is breathing freely and being comfortable with yourself.
It's fantastic to be true to yourself.

停一下，看看窗外，呼吸～～

Stop, look out the window, and breathe.

實夢小花園

檸檬馬鞭草
安神、舒緩緊張情緒。

最近腦海中常浮現兩個字「偷夢」的狀態…

夢想。是虛無飄渺的。偷的走嗎？

我想。如果沒有核心價值的去做，那麼這個夢想力是沒有生命力的…如果是好夢，利己利人的夢想，該敞開雙手，歡迎把夢想實踐吧。

流動的夢想力，傳遞愛的真諦，讓世界更美好。。

感恩造福。

The phrase "dream thief" came to my mind a lot recently.

Dreams are elusive. Can they be stolen?

I think if we go after a dream without core values, the journey won't be able to last for long. If it's a dream worth pursuing, a goal that benefits yourself and others, one should embrace it with open arms and devote oneself to realizing it.

Being brave to dream creates a constant flow that passes down the meaning of love to make the world a better place.

Appreciation brings happiness.

你有夢嗎？是什麼呢？是否在進行中呢？祝福你順著夢想前進。

Do you have dreams? What are your goals? Are you pursuing your dreams? I hope your dream will guide you move forward.

築夢小花園　／　向日葵
可降低高血壓、膽固醇、預防貧血。

作　　者：Dreamer
對　　話：林彤恩
插　　畫：Dreamer、林彤恩、W、Vi
美　　編：澹澹文化創研所
譯　　者：歐德慧

發 行 人：陳玉蓮
出　　版：賣夢工作室有限公司
地　　址：台北市文山區景華街 216 巷 6 號
電　　話：02-2930-5660
E MAIL：information@dreambubble100.com

印刷裝訂：大光華印刷
二版日期：112年10月
底　　價：NT 480 元
I S B N：978-626-95450-1-8

代理經銷 / 白象文化事業有限公司
401 台中市東區和平街 228 巷 44 號
電話：（04）2220-8589　傳真：（04）2220-8505